First published in the UK in 2008 by
QED Publishing
A Quarto Group company
226 City Road
London EC1V 2TT
www.qed-publishing.co.uk

A catalogue record for this book is available from the British Library.

ISBN 978 1 84835 078 6

Author Kate Tym
Illustrator Sarah Wade
Editor Clare Weaver
Designer Alix Wood
Consultant David Hart

Publisher Steve Evans
Creative Director Zeta Davies

Printed and bound in China

QED
MANNERS

Be
NICE

KATE TYM

Pete
the plasterer

Illustrated by Sarah Wade

Brian Boddington's family were FED UP.
Brian just didn't seem to respect **anything** or **any one**.

When Dad got a very important phone call from Mr Austere, his **very important** boss, about something **very important**, Brian played the drums... **VERY LOUDLY**.

Bongo, Brian's dog, barked along **VERY LOUDLY**, too.
Mr Austere was not impressed... and nor was Dad.

Sorry about this, Mr Austere, it's a really bad line

Pete

the plas

When Brian's teenage sister Anthea and her friend Talia wanted some private time to talk about girl things,

Brian put on his **Star-Invaders Game**, sat in the middle of them with Bongo and refused to go away.

Boys-R-Boys-R-Boys

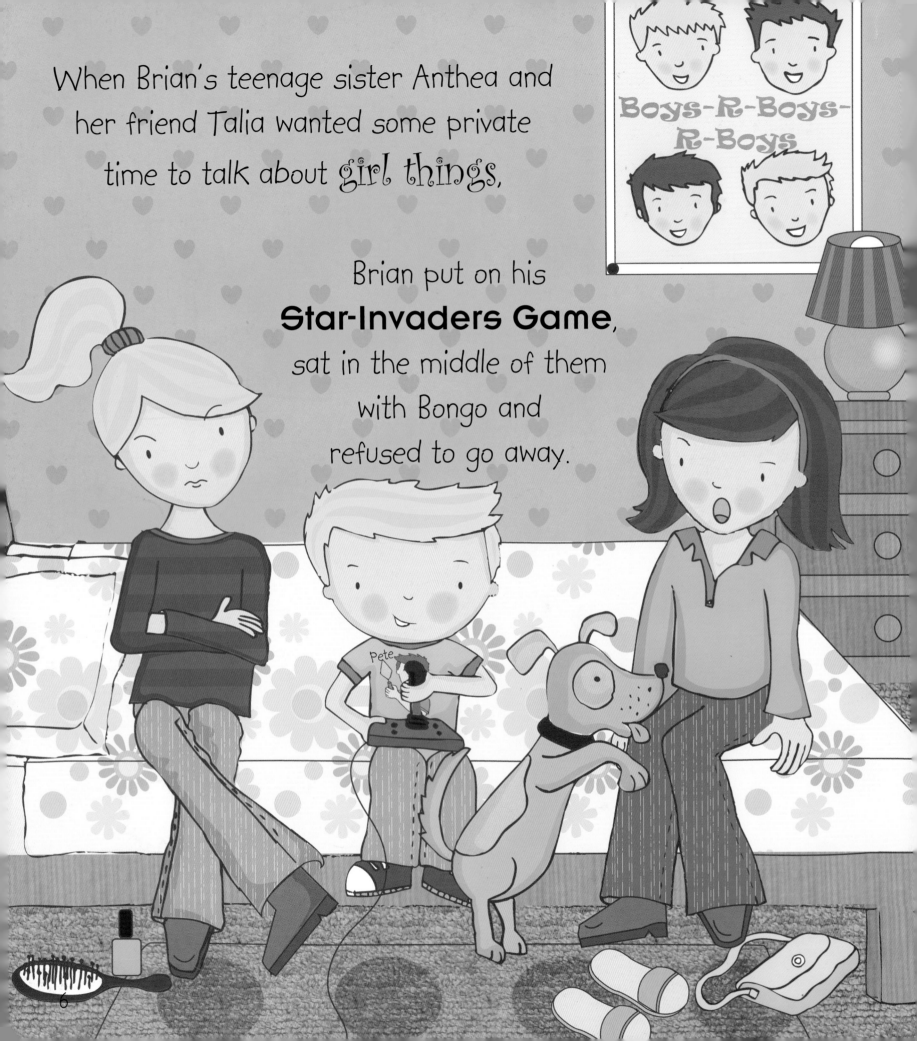

And poor old Granny never got to watch her favourite soap.
"**Budge up, Gran,**" Brian would say, patting the couch
for Bongo and grabbing the remote control.
"**It's time for Pete the Plasterer.**"

Anthea had saved up for the latest CD by her favourite band,

Boys-R-Boys-R-Boys

8

Brian was playing Frisbee in the garden with Bongo, when the Frisbee snapped in two.

"Never mind, BONGO," said Brian. "I'll find something else."

Brian walked past Anthea's room and saw her **Boys-R-Boys-R-Boys** CD glinting in its packet. "**Perfect!**" he said, taking it down to the garden and throwing it for Bongo to catch in his sharp, scratchy teeth.

Then Brian and Bongo went to the end of the garden where the old apple tree grew. The tree was loaded with delicious fruit. All Brian needed was something to get it down with. **"I know just the thing!"** he said to Bongo.

Mum found Granny
clinging to the couch
TWO HOURS later.

When Mum went to get her new silk scarf to wear on her Wednesday girls' night out, it was nowhere to be found.

But that's probably because she didn't look in Bongo's bed. **"BONGO'S lead SNAPPED,"** Brian explained later.

Mum wasn't very happy.

"BRIAN!" she shouted.

"How would you feel if we treated your things like you treat our things?" she said.

But Brian just laughed.

"You wouldn't," he said.

But then Brian made a **BIG** mistake.
He used Dad's Philippe de Fancy-Pants
Couture shirt to turn Bongo into
Super-designer Dog.
And Dad... was **MAD!**

Mum called a FAMILY MEETING
– without Brian – or Bongo.
"It's time," she said,
"to give Brian a TASTE
OF HIS OWN MEDICINE."
Everyone agreed. Even Granny!

Pete
the plasterer

Anthea "borrowed" Brian's **Star-Invaders Game** and simply "**couldn't find it**" when Brian wanted to play it.

17

Mum bought a baby-sized **Pete the Plasterer** T-shirt and pretended it was Brian's.

"Oopsy doopsy!" she said.

"It must have shrunk in the wash."

And when Brian was watching **Fabtastic Football Facts**, Granny changed channels to **OLD DOCTORS IN HOSPITAL** and sat on the remote control.

we were watching that!

Pardon dear? You'll have to speak up!

And when Brian was building **Dogopolis-mega-city** out of blocks, Dad put on one of his Old Rocker CDs so **LOUDLY** that Brian **jumped** out of his skin, knocking all the blocks over and ruining **Dogopolis** for ever.

"**DAD!**" Brian shouted, "**You ruined my game!**

What is WRONG with this family?

Anthea's lost my stuff, Mum's **ruined** my T-shirt

and even Granny's being really selfish...

Nobody treats me or my stuff with

ANY respect.

I mean, how would they feel if I took their stuff, or ruined their game or...

Oh..." said Brian.

"**Ah...**" said Brian.

"**OOPS!**" said Brian.

21

Mum called another FAMILY MEETING.
Brian said he **really was sorry**.
Everyone said they were sorry too and
gave Brian back his stuff.

And Bongo?

Bongo ate the remote control!

Oh, Bongo!

Notes for Parents and Teachers

- Look at the front cover of the book together. Talk about the picture. Can the children guess what the book is going to be about? Read the title together.

- Read page 4. Discuss with the children what it means to show someone respect. How do we treat other people's things with respect?

- Why do the children think Dad needs Brian to be quiet when he's on the phone (page 5)?

- Read page 7 together. Talk with the children about how Brian treats Granny. What do they think about the way he behaves?

- Look at pages 8–9. Anthea had saved up for her CD and bought it with her own money. Discuss with the children whether this makes what Brian does with it any worse. Anthea loves Boys-R-Boys-R-Boys. How do the children think it makes her feel when Brian takes the CD and ruins it?

- Did Brian think about the consequences of taking Granny's stick (pages 11–12)? Did he think what might happen to Granny? Discuss with the children what it means when someone behaves in a way that is 'thoughtless'.

- Does Brian ever think about other people? If he doesn't, who is he thinking about? Discuss being selfish with the children. How do other people see you if you always put your own needs first? How do other people feel about you? If Brian had asked his mum for the scarf, what would she have said (page 13)? Might she have helped Brian find something else to use? Talk through these questions and ideas with the children.

- Read page 14. Ask the children why Brian doesn't think the family would treat his things the way he treats their things. Does he really know that it wouldn't be nice to do so?

- What do the children think Mum means when she says they'll give Brian a 'taste of his own medicine' (page 16)? Can the children think of any other ways that the family could get Brian to realize how his behaviour is making them feel?

- Ask the children to look at the pictures on pages 17–19. Discuss with the children how they think Brian is feeling. Do they think he likes people using and losing his things?

- Read page 21 together. Why do the children think Brian says "Oh", "Ah" and "Oops"? What has made him realize that his family have been behaving the way he behaved? How does that make him feel?

- Do the children think Brian has learned his lesson (page 22)?

- Talk with the children about favourite things that they have. How would they feel if someone took them without asking or damaged them? Discuss the idea of treating others how you would like to be treated yourself.